Gasp!

TERRY DENTON

HA HA! They've gone next door ...

MONDO

31

Now's my chance.

Dinnertime!

Ha
Ha

°°oops!

Gasp!
No WATER.
No OXYGEN.
I can't breathe –
I've got to find
water!

27

I'm a fish out of water!

I'm dying...

AND THERE'S ONLY 27 PAGES **TO GO.**

I'm sinking...

I'm sinking...

Sink?

SINK!

Ah...

What a *brilliant* little fish I am.

NO PANIC. Stay cool.

The *sink!*

Up the cupboard,
across the bench,
to the sink...
WATER!
OXYGEN!
LIFE!

My life is so...

EMPTY!

No *water.*

Not a drop.

Gasp!

I can't breathe…

DOUBLE

Gasp!

I'm fainting.

TRIPLE

Gasp!

23

THE TOILET!

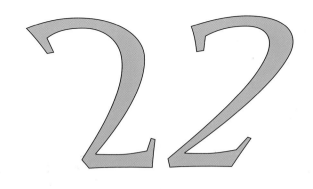

QUICK,
UP the STAIRS.
22 pages to go.
Don't
PANIC...
Keep going.

TOILET OR bUSt!

21

Lucky break.
　　Door's open ...

water!

Toilet, here I come.
Hope it's *clean* ...
　　just been *flushed!*

Toilet brush.
Another lucky break!

20

Vault upwards...

17

STOP TURNING
PAGES **PLEASE!!**

I can't breathe ...

GO BACK!

Gasp!

ONLY 17 PAGES TO GO!

Water!

Water!

I must
find
WATER.

WHAT'S
THAT
SOUND?

DRIPPING!
I hear *dripping.*
A **tap** perhaps?

You clever observant INTELLIGENT little fish.

Keep turning, reader…

The
drip
drip
drip
of a
lovely
tap.

Just
enough
water
to
keep
this
little fish
ALIVE!

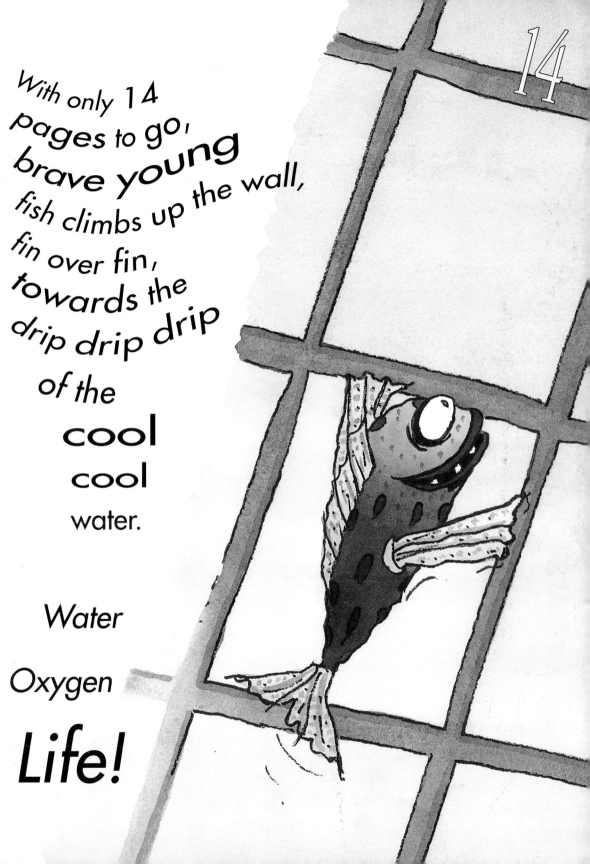

With only 14 pages to go, brave **young** fish climbs up the wall, fin over fin, towards the drip drip **drip** of the **cool** cool water.

Water

Oxygen

Life!

13

Saved by wit and cunning (and a dripping tap)

OH, CLEVER FISH ...

11

ONLY 11 TO GO!
STOP *TURNING PAGES!*
You're killing me!
GO BACK TO THE
BEGINNING, *PLEASE!*

MY LIFE'S DRAINING...

Drain...

Drain?

DRAIN?

sink

water

DRAIN

S-bend

water trap

WATER!

I'm

SAVED!!

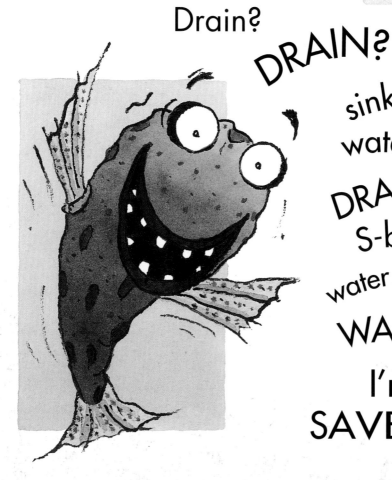

I'll just slip into the pipe, and live in the drain ... a life in the sewers ... might even be washed into a great river or lake!

OH NO!!

The grille's too fine, I can't fit through!!

9

DON'T TURN
any more pages!!
Only 9 to GO …
I'm done for.

Ga**s**p*!*

I'm slipping away.
Don't cry for me …
TURN BACK! To the beginning … **PLEASE**.
I'll be good, I won't eat the food …
I'm a good little fish … I'll be …

WHAT'S THAT?
On the roof.
A *noise* …

RAIN!

It must be RAIN.
I'm SAVED!
Turn the page,

QUICK!!

Scale
the wall,
brick
by
brick,
upward,
upward
to the
ROOF.

RAIN,

I

can
smell
RAIN.

Beautiful
moist
drippy

RAIN!!

Gasping in the rain
just gasping in the rain...

5 OH NO!
The rain's *STOPPED.*

How could you do this to me?

Gasp!

Rotten
clouds ...

COME
BACK!!

cough ...

WATER ...

oxygen ...

life ...

I'm doomed.

Only 4 pages.

So near, yet... G**a**sp!

my mind's going ... Gasp!

It's all turning black...

no oxygen... G**a**sp!

I'm slipping away... nearly made it...

but... now... Gasp! *It's too late.*

This is the END...

3

...almost.

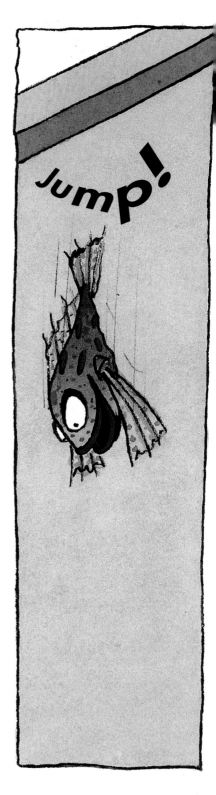

Jump!